Casina
and the
Time Portals

Casina
and the
Time Portals

C. A. Martin

Riverside Publishing Solutions

First Printing: 2019

Layout and Print:
Riverside Publishing Solutions Ltd, Salisbury
Illustrations: Nicholas Roberts

ISBN 978-1-913012-05-2

For my daughters

I should like to thank my mother, Rob,
Jean and Toni for their support
and encouragement.

In the Casina Series

Casina Beyond Time

Contents

New Eden

We are done with weed and woe
No weed, no woe, no Need
On New Eden
New dew on down,
On doe, on ewe
Nod to no one
Need no one
Wed as oNe
NOW

1

A New Planet

The road was quiet and the pavements empty: it was dusk. Casina walked along feeling furtive as she looked out for a shop that might fit the description of 'Outer Space'. She was not hopeful but to her astonishment, her gaze soon settled upon an empty shop that made her heart beat faster. The windowpane was pasted with large notices but between these could be glimpsed a dark, empty interior not, in fact, unlike Outer Space! Glinting dust motes floated in the air like dust from an asteroid belt.

The shop's name was a dead giveaway, if ever there was one: the sign above displayed the famous *Dr Who* logo. Into her mind floated an image of 'The Doctor's' Blue Police Box – The Tardis – spinning through Time and Space. She stopped outside the shop trying not to look furtive and peered through the window. She waited. Nothing happened. She wasn't sure what to expect. Determined to persevere, she moved further along the window and stopped directly in front of the unprepossessing door.

A pile of junk mail lying on the mat was clearly visible through the glass door. At that moment, she noticed the air begin to shimmer like a waterfall. Instinctively, she stepped towards it. The next moment, she found herself flying through Space and stars twinkled all around.

The speed and the wind rushing over her were exhilarating and the sight of so many millions of stars took her breath away. She noticed, with some alarm, that she was making for a small area of complete blackness that was rapidly getting larger. Just when she began to feel frightened of this looming darkness, she came to a halt. Recovering her breath and righting herself, she made out a less black area and heard a gentle humming sound.

Warily she walked towards it and then she saw a small dark ball that she could now perceive was the focus of the humming sound. Later, she described the ball as the size of a football. Well, that was how it looked to her at the time. Nothing appeared to be happening to the small ball, which stayed dark and uninteresting, with no signs of life.

Suddenly, a small object came flying through the air and landed on the ball. To her amazement, its still, dark surface began to move and heave. Pinpricks of glowing orange light appeared all over the ball from which wiggly orange lines began to run. Soon, the ball was covered in a network of bright orange lines as though held in a fishing net.

Looking more carefully, she could just make out that the pinpricks were spurting jets of orange light and, at that moment, a sound reached her ears. She gasped. Could it be! Surely not! Was this small sphere a planet and were the orange dots and moving ribbons really volcanoes that were erupting and sending out rivers of fiery lava?

A sense of awe and wonder came over her and she stood spellbound, waiting to see what would unfold. She realised she was watching nothing less than the creation of a new planet, just as her friend Steve said she would.

The humming continued steadily as if sustaining the new planet. Casina perceived that Eons of Time passed as the black and orange surface of the planet continued to heave and shift. Then all grew still again. More time, beyond count, passed as the planet appeared to cool.

Suddenly, in a twinkling, the ball turned blue with one large circle of green set in the midst of the blue, 'like an emerald,' thought Casina. It was as if someone had waved a magic wand. Looking more closely at the green land – for that is what it was – Casina observed it was mostly covered in trees. But there were also mountains, lakes, rivers and grass-land. Tiny puffs of white appeared and began moving. Casina realised they were clouds. Oh, it was beautiful!

She knew the act of creation had been completed when the humming ceased. The instant she understood this, she was enveloped in a 'whooshing' sound, and the next moment she found herself back on the pavement. Trying to look casual, she calmly turned away from the door of the *Dr Who* shop and walked slowly along the street, crossed the road, and turned into the lane where she lived.

Her friend Steve had been right after all! There really were Time Portals in our world hidden under our very noses. He had told her – with a meaningful look not lost on Casina – that, sometimes, they were concealed in shop entrances. The reason for this is the name of the shop provides a vital clue as to the traveller's destination, but it is the seeker's intention that unlocks the Portal. She couldn't wait to tell him of her adventure when they met tomorrow, as agreed, in the public gardens nearby.

2

Garden of Eden

Steve's appearance was deceptive. He was short with stooping shoulders, a weather beaten face and small, bright blue eyes. The scruffy impression was largely due to his attire, which consisted of a shapeless, blue cotton jacket with cap to match, so that he resembled a worker from Communist China. His voice was surprisingly deep and comforting, due to the Wiltshire accent, and he had a cheerful manner. At his side, trotted his tousled terrier who was called Shay, as in 'shaman', Steve explained. He often walked with a sturdy walking stick that was so tall it qualified as a Wizard's Staff.

She spied him and Shay in the distance crossing the bridge from the water meadows.

Casina waved; she was dying to tell him about her 'Dr Who' experience. His eyes twinkled in his lined, leathery face as he asked how she was.

"You were right" she couldn't help blurting out. "I found the Portal; it just appeared and there I was, in Outer Space." She would have continued but Steve interrupted quietly;

"And now the serious stuff can begin."

Casina was taken aback but before she could reply, he went on:

"Now that you have seen for yourself that Time Portals do exist, you can travel back in Time to correct some of the anomalies set in train by the Big Bang. Take the Garden of Eden for instance; what is the meaning of the Snake? You have an opportunity to change the original script if you go back to that Beginning. Do you follow the original script or write a new one? A chance – a glance through the Window of Time as it stands very still – no thought upon it – Snake – Green Lady – Pieces of Eight. Find the right doorway and, don't worry, help will appear when needed.

"Oh, and you will need someone to guard the entrance when you go through. Now you have been through once, those on the Dark Side have been alerted and they will try to slip through with you at your next attempt and thwart you. You might think of enlisting your mother's help."

He changed the subject and Casina, putting aside the puzzle with which Steve had presented her, found herself slipping easily into everyday conversation before they went their separate ways.

Where, Casina and her mother wondered, was the most likely location for the Portal to take Casina back in Time to the Beginning of the Garden of Eden? They went through a number of possibilities until they remembered that nearby Wilton House had once played host to the Elizabethan courtier, Sir Philip Sydney who, inspired by the beauty of the surrounding valley and downs, had written his book, *Arcadia*.

The book harkened back to the Greek and Roman ideal of an Earthly Paradise, where life was beautiful and everyone got on with each other, just as they had in the Garden of Eden before things went wrong. If Wilton was the original setting for this Heaven on Earth, they felt sure the doorway must be nearby.

They hit upon the idea of the Wilton Garden Centre as being a very possible location as it was right next to Wilton House. The same river that flowed through the Wilton House Estate, flowed past the Garden Centre. Naturally, there was public access and, best of all, you were inconspicuous in amongst the plants and foliage!

Casina and her mother set off at the first opportunity on an afternoon when the sun was shining. The Garden Centre looked as beautiful as ever, framed as it is by the trees of the Wilton Estate. They were wandering down in the direction of the river when both saw the arch at the same time.

A white clematis was growing up the arched frame and there was something about it that drew them irresistibly. Sure enough, as they came closer, the air seen through the arch began to shimmer. Casina's mother whispered to her to go through quickly whilst she watched her back.

Casina stepped through and found herself in a forest suffused with a soft, glowing, green light, and her senses were at once assailed by the delicious aroma of damp earth and vegetation. Then it hit her. There were no sounds: not a bird sang, not a leaf moved. There was an all-pervading air of stillness. She remembered Steve's words about the Garden of Eden *'standing very still'*. All at once, Casina realised she was back in that Garden, before Time began, when the Earth was newly made and waiting for life to appear.

She thought of what else he had said – something to do with a Snake and a Green Lady. The Green Lady had to be Eve. Wasn't it a Snake that had tempted Eve to eat of the Forbidden Fruit of the Tree that stood at the centre of the Garden of Eden – or so the story went? She hoped that if she found the Snake that it, too, would be frozen like everything else in the forest.

She wandered through this eerie idyll, content for the moment to enjoy the beauty of the trees and sparkling streams and to inhale the cool, refreshing air. Then she saw them;

the Snake and the Green Lady, together, gazing lovingly at one another. The Snake was enormous and seemed to be part of the earth so that the trees appeared to be growing along its back. Standing sideways on, just in front of the Snake, thus obscuring part of its head, was the Green Lady, Eve. Her hair was in a ponytail and she was expecting a baby. Casina blinked to make sure she was seeing properly. She was seeing correctly: Eve's body formed part of the Snake's head. They were joined. How odd!

Somehow, she understood the significance of this still moment in Time. The Snake was Eve's Other Self and they were still connected, although, she thought with alarm, they were beginning to pull apart and separate. Duality had not yet been born and could still be prevented from happening. What must she do to change the script in this precious moment?

Something out of place in the scene caught her eye. To her left, leaning incongruously against the trunk of a tree, was a small blackboard with words written on it in white chalk.

She walked over to have a peer and, as she knelt down, she noticed a matchbox on the grass, which she picked up.

The words on the blackboard were as follows:

Strike the Spark of Life
A tinderbox can be struck
Once
To create a spark
So that two sparks won't fly

She thought the tinderbox somewhat poetic as she regarded the Bryant & May matches in her hand, but she could be in no doubt as to what she was to do. There must only be the one spark – and not a second one – so that Duality would not be born. The Snake was the symbol for the aberration that was Duality with its forked tongue and split eye.

However, she was forgetting the other clue, *'Pieces of Eight'*. At home, Casina had given this enigmatic phrase some thought. In the context of the Green Snake, the 's' at the end of 'Pieces' is the symbol for a snake, whilst the number '8' can be described as being an 'S' joined with its reflection, or shadow-self.

The expression itself is notoriously associated with pirates and their lust for gold ducats, doubloons or, 'Pieces of Eight'. In other words, the phrase is a metaphor for greed.

When the Snake is united with its reflection, or shadow-self, the 'S' is automatically removed from the word 'Pieces' because it has been turned into an '8', so 'Piece' now sounds like 'Peace'. '8' is also the symbol for Infinity when laid on its side. As we know, Infinity means going on and on forever and having no end.

The original phrase has now become, 'Peace of Infinity'. The Good and Bad, as shown us by the two Eves – Green Lady and Snake, have been reunited. We can live in peace and harmony in the Garden of Eden – forever.

Resolutely, Casina stood up and, taking a match out of the box, struck the match. In an instant, everything changed. The forest became swathed in mist, the Snake and Eve were lost from view and the great forest became filled with sound. Casina was awed by the primeval feeling in the air. Gradually, a faint light began to appear through the mist as the sun rose ever higher. It felt as if the world was newly born.

As the mist began to disperse, Casina wandered slowly through the forest with the uncomfortable feeling that she had not quite accomplished what Steve expected of her. In a small clearing, she saw a peacock and thought to herself, 'I really am in Paradise'. The bird had an object in its beak, which, on closer inspection, turned out to be a dead snake. She took it as a sign that indeed the Snake was no more.

A beautiful young woman entered the glade with flowers threaded in her long golden hair. What was so extraordinary was that she was golden all over. Her golden skin glowed and her eyes shone with pure joy as she skipped past Casina. There could be no mistaking that she was Eve, but she was green no longer.

"I must now plant my garden," she trilled happily as she put her hand into a pocket and drew out a handful of seeds.

"I will scatter them on the river so they can reach all four corners of the Garden." And with that she was gone, laughing merrily.

Finally, Casina realised what had been nagging at her: she wished to see The Tree in the Garden of Eden. She felt it would show her that she had got things right. Most importantly, she wished to see with her own eyes that the Snake, traditionally entwined around the trunk, was no longer there, nor lurking nearby.

She continued walking until she entered a large circular clearing in the forest and, at its centre, stood The Tree of Life at the centre of the Garden of Eden. Casina had the impression that the trees on the perimeter were leaning lovingly in towards this magnificent tree laden with golden apples for, like Eve, it too, was no longer green but golden.

Of course, Casina new the old stories of myth and legend that say, *In the very Beginning, there was a Golden Age where the inhabitants were never ill nor did they grow old.*' It had been downhill ever since. We fell from grace into the *Silver Age* and then the *Bronze Age* and finally our present time, the *Iron Age.*

She could see that the Snake, as well as those other creatures shut out in the Darkness of Duality, would have felt excluded from the glory and beauty of the Light and who, out of spite, would have wished to destroy that bliss. It all made perfect sense. Now we were back at the Beginning of a New Creation, in a new Golden Age and the Snake was no more so that the Golden Age would go on and on.

Wandering back through the forest, she suddenly glimpsed the Golden Eve kneeling beside a river. She seemed to be concentrating very hard on something in her lap, and she was singing. Overcome with curiosity, Casina walked towards her. As she drew closer, she recognised the song, a well-known nursery rhyme which goes thus:

I had a little nut tree

Nothing would it bear

But a silver nutmeg

And a golden pear

As Casina emerged from the wood, Eve looked up and smiled.

"Do you like my golden apple tree?"

"It's very pretty", Casina replied.

"The apples on the Golden Tree are just like the fruit of the Little Nut Tree, except that each fruit contains a mixture of both the golden pear and the silver nutmeg. That is why the King of Spain's daughter will soon be visiting."

Casina could quite see why the Spanish Princess would want to cross the wide seas to visit such a magnificent golden tree with such fruit. Eve went back to fiddling with what looked like string in her lap. Finally, she let out a cry of frustration.

"Perhaps you will help me?" she asked Casina. "I am trying to make a human body with this twine but it keeps springing out of my hand." As she looked up, Casina could clearly see that Eve's eyes were golden with green flecks.

"I will do my best", Casina replied dubiously, wondering how one made a body out of garden twine, for she could now see that that is what the string was. Curiously, it was rusty red, rather than the usual green beloved of gardeners.

Eve explained what she was trying to do. The twisted twine was the Human DNA of the 'Twins'. She wished to make the Twins – one male, the other female – into One Being by tying each end of the length of twine together to make a circle. Eve explained she wished to 'tie a butterfly', which Casina realised was Eve's way of saying 'tie a bow'. Firstly, it would look prettier than a knot and, secondly, it would neatly demonstrate the two small circles of the bow, or man and woman, becoming the one large circle. 'Perhaps this is what was meant to have happened in the First Beginning?' Casina thought to herself. 'Were the different sex bodies never meant to have been?'

While Casina held the twine down with her forefinger, Eve finally managed to make a bow and was highly delighted with the result. She arose thanking Casina and saying she must go and tend her garden. Casina set off once again, attempting to retrace her steps. She trudged on and on, thinking there had to be an easier way to get back when, all of a sudden, she saw a large expanse of shimmering air and knew this was her way out.

The next minute she found herself back in the Wilton Garden Centre on the other side of the arch, as if she had never left. Her mother gave her a keen, inquiring look and remarked that she had disappeared from view when she walked through the arch but that she had reappeared only a split second later.

3

The Shadow World

"**Y**ou have also created a Wasteland," Steve calmly replied. Casina had been telling Steve all about her experiences in the Garden of Eden as they walked along the footpath by the river.

"You missed the clues. Didn't you see the Tatterdemalians in the shadows of the trees? There was also another clue", he added.

"What are Tatterdemalians?" Casina asked, then thinking better of it, she added quickly, "Don't worry; I'll look it up when I get home".

Trying hard to disguise her disappointment and confusion, they walked on in silence until Steve suggested that she had better do what Alice in Wonderland did, and go through the

Looking Glass. Casina was more confused than ever.

A few days later, she finished reading Lewis Carroll's *Alice Through the Looking Glass*, and, as she put the book down, the germ of an idea began to form in her mind: there really was a mirror, or shadow world which was the opposite of our world, and the Tatterdemalians were part of it. The English Dictionary's definition of the word was *a person dressed in ragged clothes*, whilst Thesaurus writes: *a dirty, shabbily clothed urchin.* Thesaurus also suggested: *broken-down, dilapidated, ramshackle, derelict, tumble-down, bedraggled.*

The meaning was unequivocal: tatterdemalions were the rejected people in society, forced to live their pitiful lives in the shadows, mostly out of sight. This was why she had failed to notice their silent presence in the shadows of the trees.

In Alice's mirror world in Lewis Carroll's book, you experience the opposite of what we are used to finding in the visible world. Hence, when Alice went through the Looking Glass, she discovered she needed to run in order to stay in the same place and, in order to reach her desired destination, she had to set off in the opposite direction to the one she wanted to go in.

Then it dawned on her that the reason for the Shadow World being left out, or marginalised, could surely be traced back to the original experiment that was the Big Bang.

Her mind had fairly boggled when she first heard such a momentous event as the Beginning of Time being called 'an experiment', which, furthermore, had gone awry practically straightaway. It was this that had caused the Dark to separate from the Light. Trying to make sense of everything, it seemed to Casina that, although she had prevented Eve's Shadow self from splitting away i.e. her Snake self, the Garden itself had also been separated. Steve was showing her that this anomaly also needed to be put right.

Somehow, she must find a way of uniting the two halves of the Garden of Eden. On the one hand there was the desolation of The Wasteland and on the other, the beautifully scented Garden teeming with all manner of life.

Casina smiled. She already knew where the next Time Portal was most likely to be – the shop called *Alice's in Wonderland*. It sold dancing gear that included a lot of pink-and-white items such as pink ballet pumps and white tutus. Appropriately, therefore, the shop front was painted in wide pink and white candy stripes. The effect was somewhat outrageous, particularly as the doors were reminiscent of the swing doors of a saloon bar in an American movie of the Wild West. She wondered if the shop had a looking glass like the one Alice went through, but she never did find out.

If there had been someone from the Opposition following them in the Wilton Garden Centre, Casina and her mother had been unaware of them. Even more reason, they felt, to be extra vigilant as they set out for *Alice's in Wonderland*. They both scanned the length of the lane, which, luckily, happened to be empty. As they reached the top, prior to crossing the main road, her mother turned to look behind them and saw, to her horror, a very thin man with narrow shoulders, thin flaxen hair and small eyes who was looking directly at them: and those eyes were hard and humourless.

"Don't turn round, but there is someone behind us."

They had to wait a tantalising few seconds before being able to cross the road, by which time the person was standing right next to Casina. As they crossed, Casina's mother stepped between her and the man. They stopped outside the window of the pink and white shop to see what their pursuer would do. Brazenly, he stopped too.

Without exchanging a word Casina and her mother went into action. Casina began walking towards the entrance to the shop whilst her mother followed her, walking backwards and never taking her eyes off the man, ready to stop him physically if necesssary. He stood still, clearly not wanting to create a scene. Casina saw the shimmering light and stepped through into another world.

She found herself in what was unmistakably a municipal park. There were the different shaped flowerbeds ablaze with colour, as well as the neatly mown grass and trimmed hedges. She then realised what was out of place with the scene. Although the flowers were blooming, people were dressed in winter clothes.

'Oh my goodness,' she thought, 'I really have gone through Alice's Looking Glass and everything is the opposite of what it should be.'

For a while, she stood where she was merely observing the surroundings until she noticed something odd in the people's behaviour. Every now and then someone would stop and place their hands over a flower bed, noticeably relax, or give a shiver, before walking on.

'What on earth are they doing', Casina thought to herself.

Nothing loath, she went up boldly to a young mother holding the hands of two small children and asked politely why people were putting their hands over the flower beds. Casina could see the mother was surprised by what she clearly thought an obvious question.

She replied: "When people's hands are cold, they warm them up by holding them over the red flowers, or when they are feeling mentally sluggish, say, they hold them over a patch of yellow flowers." Warming to the subject she went on: "Or if they wish to improve their concentration they look for indigo coloured flowers. If you want to…"

"Oh, I see." Casina interrupted, seeing this helpfulness might stretch too far. She tried to sound casual, although her mind was reeling from the explanation.

She thanked the woman and, wishing to show that she was quite normal really, said she was a visitor to the town and where might she find The Wasteland please. Looking visibly relieved, the woman smiled and pointed Casina in the right direction.

Fortunately, although it was May in her world, Casina was wearing a jacket so did not stand out too much from the winter-clad inhabitants. She couldn't make out whether the temperature was warm or cold so gave up on the conundrum.

Exiting the park, she found herself walking down the main street of a small town with the usual shops. She had been informed that The Wasteland was to be found where a building project of a block of flats had stalled due to the recession.

Turning off the main road, she walked through a covered entrance between a row of Victorian buildings. This led into a long court-yard with an old mill at the far end. On her left was The Wasteland. A modest block of flats was to have been built there to fill a vacant, urban space but work had scarcely begun before being abandoned. This had clearly been some months' ago because a desolate feeling hung over the place like a pall.

Casina peered through the high wire fencing which separated her from that desolate place and the tidy, organised world where she stood. Piles of orange-coloured builder's sand lay like slag heaps in several places, and tall grasses had grown in uneven clumps. Just at that moment, a rat darted out into a small patch of open land before scurrying into the long grass. Staring more intently at the scene, she noticed how broken branches from the straggly hedging of the railway embankment lay on the ground like writhing snakes.

Unsurprisingly perhaps, there was a large 'FOR SALE' sign on the land, whilst on Casina's side of the fence, she noticed a large

'SOLD' sign in front of a small business. An idea began to form in her mind, but how to put it into effect?

Each sign was mutually exclusive of the other, i.e. a place couldn't be 'For Sale' if it was 'Sold', and vice versa. If she could somehow combine the two, that should do it. She was startled by a voice coming out of nowhere.

"Does your right hand know what the left hand is doing?" Casina looked around to see where the voice was coming from. There was no one there.

"Over here, silly," the voice urged.

She looked in the direction where she thought the sound might have come from and her eyes rested on the 'SOLD' Sign. To her utter amazement, she noticed a pair of pale, watery blue eyes, a nose and a mouth on the board, which were very much alive.

Once she had got over the shock of a talking sign, she asked it to explain what it meant by its remark. Articulating very carefully the Sign repeated what it had just said. Casina had to stifle a laugh and compose her features as the Sign looked so ridiculous carefully pursing its lips to make the individual sounds.

"If your right hand does not know what the left hand is doing, that means the left hand does not know what the right hand is doing, but if you bring the palms of both hands together, then they will each know what the other is doing."

"Why, that's how I can unite the two Signs," Casina said. She realised Steve was right: she was given clues when she needed them.

Feeling relieved and excited at the same time, she thanked the Talking Sign effusively. "Thank you, thank you. By bringing the palms of my hands together The Wasteland will cease to exist."

"You have already done it," said the Sign in a superior voice.

"No, I haven't."

"Yes, you have."

She was just about to contradict him again when she stopped herself, realising that this was becoming childish.

"Well, I am going to do it anyway," she replied stubbornly.

Imagining that her left hand was the 'FOR SALE' Sign and that her right hand was the 'SOLD' Sign, she slowly began moving the palms together. The atmosphere around her became still, expectant, and the sounds of everyday life muted. As her palms met, the fencing, the buildings and the derelict land all fell away. She felt herself swept backwards through a tunnel but instead of finding herself on the pavement, as she fully expected, she found herself elsewhere.

4

Valentine's Day

This time, judging by the enormous castle in the distance, she must be in the formal gardens of a French Chateau. As she adjusted herself to this new environment, she realised that the gardens were vast – square upon square of low, neatly trimmed box hedging, containing patterns of hearts, diamonds, clubs and spades. Topiary trees of a spiral design stood sentinel at the entrances. However, what could not fail to attract attention was that the vegetation was not green but a golden yellow, and the flowers filling the patterns were sugar pink. The most popular pattern within the squares were pairs of hearts with the tops touching each other and the tips pointing away.

She was in a sunken area, so decided to climb the stone steps to get a better view. The gardens were impressive, if somewhat bizarre, given the golden vegetation. She wondered if Eve's new Garden of Eden had anything to do with it.

Stretched out before her was a large lake surrounded by a wide tree-lined, gravel path. Walking along the avenue of trees, she crossed a small bridge where the water from the lake overflowed into a stream with small bridges criss-crossing all the way down. The water made a pretty burbling sound as it flowed down the steps beneath the bridges.

Coming back to her senses, Casina was wondering if she was completely alone in the garden when a man came running along the gravel path towards her. He was dressed in red and gold breeches with a gold braided jacket to match. A white wig with sausage-roll curls either side of a centre parting, and a small pony-tail at the back with a black bow, completed the outfit. He looked remarkably like a footman who has lost his gilded carriage. Addressing her in an urgent, breathless voice, he uttered:

"Perhaps you can help? We are so worried. The King and Queen have turned pink and refuse to rule anymore. They just sit in the rose arbour gazing into each other's eyes. What is to be done?"

Feeling flattered she was being asked to help in such a serious matter, Casina replied that she was not sure she could be of any assistance but she would gladly visit Their Majesties. The footman proceeded to lead her through the formal gardens until they came to a screen of tall hedging. They turned to follow the line of the hedge until, to Casina's alarm, the footman disappeared from view. He had slipped through a concealed entrance and Casina anxiously followed.

She found herself in the most beautiful garden filled with flowers and butterflies and the soft cooing of doves, which she could see in the boughs of the trees. At the far end of the golden lawn, she espied a swinging seat in a rose covered arbour where the king and queen sat holding hands and gazing at each other.

As she walked with the footman towards the royal couple – Casina with some trepidation

– she caught sight of a glinting object at the edge of a flowerbed. It was a jewel-encrusted crown that must have been discarded by either one of Their Majesties.

On reaching the edge of the arbour, the footman cleared his throat loudly whereupon the King and Queen turned towards him, still holding hands.

"I have brought this lady to advise your Majesties." The King and Queen turned a solemn gaze on Casina who asked how she might be of assistance.

They gave a collective sigh and replied in unison:

"We have been like this ever since we turned pink. We used to be three people each – one white, one red and one black but now we have become one person each and it is quite blissful. But we do so long to unite our two hearts."

Casina's mind was rapidly sifting through what she could remember of the story of *Alice in Wonderland* and she could only recall a white king and queen and a red pair, but not black. Of course! Red and white when mixed together make pink!

"Excuse me, but are you sure there was a black king and queen?" Casina asked politely.

"Oh yes, they were just hiding. But can't you tell? They give extra lustre to the wonderful shade of pink we have become."

It was true; the shade of pink was quite beautiful. Remembering her recent experiences, Casina cast about thinking of how she might help the King and Queen become One Heart.

Her eyes fell upon a small round table to one side of the swinging seat, which was set as if for Valentine's Day. There was an ice bucket with a bottle of champagne, two champagne flutes and a large heart-shaped box of chocolates that had been opened but left untouched with the lid lying at a rakish angle.

"I see it is Valentine's Day today", Casina commented to give herself time, although an idea was already forming in her mind.

"It is always Valentine"s Day, ever since we turned pink that is. Now you can understand our yearning."

With a burst of clarity Casina replied: "Why, all you need do is each take one half of the heart box and unite the Two Halves. That should do it."

The King and Queen grasped eagerly at this solution and without hesitation the King passed the lid to his wife, for he was the nearest to the table, picked up the bottom tray himself, and tipped the chocolates unceremoniously on to the grass.

The King and Queen then rose to their feet and, facing each other, with great concentration and solemnity, slowly brought the two halves of the chocolate box together.

As the lids came together, the King and Queen began to merge, at which point the footman fainted, and Casina felt a familiar rushing sound in her ears and the scene began to fade away. The next moment she really was standing on the pavement outside the pink ballet shop.

5

The Heart Key

Steve and Casina were sitting on a bench by the river overlooking the tranquil water meadows. Shay was busy snuffling in the long grasses by the river's edge. It was late afternoon and the sun's rays cast a golden light over the meadows and trees. Casina had just finished relating her adventures to Steve and was waiting for a response.

"Good, we can now move on to the next phase," he replied. There was silence for a moment while Casina took this on board.

"What is the next phase, please?" she replied, her mind racing.

"It is time to raise the planet's vibration." he replied simply. "As you know, after the cataclysms that caused the sinking of Atlantis, the planet's vibrations fell so that the survivors woke up to a very different world. It is time for us to return to the higher frequency. Do you fancy a trip to Egypt to see the Great Pyramid of Giza?" he said, turning towards Casina with a quizzical smile.

Taken unawares, Casina found herself saying, "Yes". Her mind was already filling with images of the Great Pyramid in the sand and of a setting sun. She had always wanted to go to Egypt and would dearly love to experience the sheer size of that extraordinary structure. Then she realised Steve must have something specific in mind.

"It is good to taste the world," he continued. "Of course, you will need to state your destination; otherwise you might end up at the North Pole. And you will need this."

From his capacious pocket, he produced a small purple, drawstring-bag. There was lettering on both sides that read 'Hi Ho' and there was a picture of an old-fashioned aeroplane climbing steeply out of a loop-the-loop.

Peering into the bag Casina saw it was lined with purple satin and contained a large, polished, milky-white crystal.

"It holds the key," was all he would say in answer to the question on her face. He stood up and Casina knew that their conversation was at an end, and that she and her mother would have to work the rest out for themselves. A few pleasantries were exchanged along the lines of how well the roses were doing in the Gardens and how Steve had discovered an adder's nest on the river walk behind the industrial estate.

Casina strolled home. Slipping the crystal out of its bag, she saw that it was in the shape of a heart and had a beautiful sheen on its smooth milky-white surface. The Internet informed her it was the crystal known as Selenium and some of its properties caught her attention – that it quickly *disperses accumulated negativity*. As well as helping ground the higher frequencies, it '... *is one of the best stones with which to bring about a rapid shift of energy.*' (Berenice Watt).

She noticed there was a large, clear 'blemish' at the centre. On closer inspection, she saw that it was in the shape of a key! Steve had said the crystal held the key and indeed it did! The 'bow' of the key – the part you hold to turn the key in the lock – was diamond-shaped – not the kind you wear on an engagement finger, but the diamond suit in a deck of cards, say. Or you could also describe it as a triangle meeting its reflection and, for that matter, the Great Pyramid joined to its reflection.

She felt it was important to know where Egypt was in relation to the rest of the world. A world map gave a view of the globe in a flattened state so that the landmasses could all be seen on one page. To her amazement, she saw that Egypt sat at the very centre. Perhaps that was why the crystal key was heart-shaped.

That evening Casina filled her mother in on the latest developments. Her mother was intrigued by the Selenium crystal and examined it closely. She let out a gasp and called Casina over excitedly saying there was a pyramid within the crystal.

Looking through the translucent area on the stone, a three-dimensional landscape emerged. It was of a long, steep-sided valley and there, in the valley, stood a large pyramid! Casina and her mother were awestruck by this further detail, in addition to all the others

– the crystal being heart-shaped and Egypt being at the 'heart' of the world's land mass and, finally, the properties of the crystal itself.

The only connection they could think of between the 'key' and the Great Pyramid was that the 'key' was meant to unlock something. They knew that the Great Pyramid was built after the misuse of the power of a Great Crystal on Atlantis, which resulted in the destruction of that fabled island in the middle of the Atlantic Ocean. It had also caused the Earth's energy level to fall. The construction of the Great Pyramid was designed to prevent such a calamity ever occurring again.

In that case, the Great Pyramid was intimately linked to the Earth's energy level or harmonic note. It could be no coincidence that such a large structure, one made to very precise measurements with remarkable properties in the King's Chamber (an object placed there does not perish), was constructed of stone because 'stone' contains the words TONE and NOTE.

Although they did not know how Casina was to use the 'Heart Key', they did at least know where to find the next Portal that would take her to the Great Pyramid. Steve had kindly dropped a clue. At the top of the lane was a road and on the opposite side was a shop called, *Taste the World*. Casina remembered that Steve had remarked it was good to 'taste the world'.

"Let's do it tomorrow as I am free in the morning," her mother suggested impulsively. Casina readily agreed and, mid-morning of the following day, found the pair of them standing outside the delicatessen gazing up at the large letters of, *Taste the World*.

Instinctively, they both turned to scan the street in both directions. Just at that moment, a large public bus drew away from the bus stop opposite revealing a young woman clad in black, wearing heavy black boots and with long dark hair piled messily on top of her head. She was staring aggressively at Casina and her mother.

"I don't like the look of her. Quickly, go through the Portal now." As her mother spoke, the woman began to cross the road making directly for them. The happy calm of just moments ago was gone as Casina turned around and stepped purposefully towards the door of the shop and said, "Egypt", out loud. Fortunately, she began to experience the tingling, shimmering effect and the grey street and drab colours fell away to be replaced by dazzling sunlight.

Casina found herself on the shore of a wide brown river. She was standing on dry dusty earth beneath a palm tree and the brilliant dappled sunlight danced in the light breeze blowing off the river. She stood still, happily absorbing the beautiful surroundings when she suddenly noticed an Arab in long striped clothes and turban standing by a palm tree not fifty feet away. He turned towards Casina and gave a slight bow which she found herself reciprocating. With his hands in his sleeves, he walked slowly towards Casina and then stopped when he was still some distance away, 'so as not to alarm me' she found herself thinking.

"Greetings," he said, smiling. "I believe you wish to visit the Great Pyramid and have brought the Heart of the Mountain with you."

Casina was non-plussed. How did he know the purpose of her visit and, for that matter, what was the 'Heart of the Mountain'? Then she understood: it was the crystal heart key.

"Thank you for your greetings. You are right; I do have the Heart of the Mountain with me," she called out. "Can you take me to the Great Pyramid by any chance?"

"Of course, that is why I am here: I was told you were coming."

He now came closer and looked at her with calm, clear brown eyes. "Give me your hand and I will take you there." Unhesitatingly, she placed her hand in his and, as if it were the most natural thing in the world, he began to rise from the ground, taking Casina with him before she had time to doubt she would be able to follow. Soon they were travelling, or rather, levitating, over a vast plain of cultivated green and brown fields.

"Won't people find it strange to see us flying through the air", she commented.

"They can't see us: we are invisible to their eyes as we are not wholly part of their world. We breathe a finer air."

At length, a streak of yellow land appeared on the horizon that steadily increased in size. They were nearing the great Plateau of Giza on which the Great Pyramid had been built. Some years ago, it was discovered that the three largest pyramids on the plateau – the largest of which is the Great Pyramid – reflected the alignment of the three stars in the belt of the Constellation of Orion. These three pyramids now became visible and Casina's excitement mounted.

All of a sudden, Casina was almost blinded by a flash of bright light. Where was it coming from? Her guide shifted direction and the blinding light was gone. When she next looked she gasped in astonishment. The Pyramid was clad all over in white stone: it must have been the sunlight bouncing off the white surface that had blinded her. They were now hovering directly above the pinnacle, except that Casina could see that the tip was in reality a small platform. Slowly they descended.

"Do you know what to do?" her guide asked.

Casina had to confess she did not. "But I know the Heart Key, er, Heart of the Mountain is a key, so presumably I need to turn it in a lock."

"Yes, it is the turning that is the important part," the Arab eagerly agreed. "But by how much do you turn the key?" he asked, as if probing her knowledge. Casina thought about this for a moment.

"Well, you usually put a key in upright and then turn it to the right.... I suppose that's 90°."

Her guide agreed, and went on to say that the turning of the key needed to be very precise as the 90° turn resulted in just the right raise in frequency – neither too much nor too little.

This is why, in ancient times, Initiates of the Mystery Schools walked the maze, which included four right-angled turns – left, right, left, right. Each 90° turn was associated with the raising of their consciousness, or understanding of the world.

He also explained that the Earth's magnetic poles had changed four times and that they had all been by 90°. However, each time there had been a fall in the planet's frequency. This time, using the fantastic device that was the Great Pyramid, the Earth's harmonic frequency could be tuned higher.

"Are you saying that the 'lock' is the Great Pyramid itself ?"

"In a manner of speaking," came the reply. "The Heart of the Mountain is showing you that it is indeed the key that is to be used on the Great Pyramid because it contains an image of the pyramid at its centre. By the way, you do realise that the Pyramid is in the shape of a diamond, and not just a triangle. The base of the visible structure is joined to another, upside-down pyramid deep in the Earth. Is there a diamond on the Crystal?" He enquired.

Casina said there was, and showed him the diamond-shape of the key 'bow' on the white crystal. He appeared satisfied.

"All that remains is to turn the Key in the Lock."

Somehow, Casina knew what to do. She moved to the centre of the platform, bent down and, with the thought of raising the Diamond Pyramid's resonance by a Note, touched the white platform with the tip of the Crystal Heart. Carefully, as if it were a key, she turned the crystal from right to left through 90°. A tremor ran through the vast edifice.

Once again, her Guide took her hand. They rose into the air and were soon speeding back towards the River Nile. Standing on its banks with the light dancing all around them, her Guide motioned her towards a space beside one of the trees. Casina knew it was the entrance that would take her back to her world. They exchanged thanks and she turned and waved as she stepped through the invisible gateway. She was sucked through with a rushing sound and almost instantly found herself back in the gloomy English light.

Casina reappeared staring at her mother's back and instantly remembered the woman in black who was making straight for them. She quickly stepped forwards, away from the Time Portal, in the hope that that would ensure it was now closed. They both stood side by side and watched the woman reach the pavement. She was glaring at them with open hostility but she looked away as she reached them, and continued walking down the street. The danger was over.

"You are not going to believe what happened...' and Casina began her story.

Later on, she met up with Steve and told him all about her experience, all over again. As ever, his reply took her by surprise.

6

The Green Dragon

"That is just the start. The planet has shifted gear which means the energy system that was laid out over her surface needs retuning. The Green Dragon has been ailing for a long time and is now very sick. She must be revived."

"How can that be done?" Casina asked in an alarmed voice, thinking that reviving dragons might be a hazardous business.

Calmly, and a little smugly, Casina thought, Steve delved into his pocket and took out an old-fashioned child's xylophone. Once upon a time, it must have been very colourful but now the eight metal keys were dented and held only traces of the rainbow colours.

"This will help you. Oh, I nearly forgot the mallet." And he retrieved one from the other pocket.

"Aren't there usually two?"

"You will only need one."

When Steve called Shay to his side, Casina knew she was going to receive no further information but she already knew where the next Time Portal was.

Once again, Casina and her mother set off on foot from Casina's home. This time the shop was further along the street towards the town centre, on the busy side. Soon they were standing outside a restaurant called *The Dragon* which, like the 'Loathly Worm' itself, was long and low and occupied the first floors of two small, old houses. The name stood out, written as it was in large white letters on a brown background, with Chinese writing at either end. The pavement was clogged with passers-by.

They decided to wait until the coast became clear; as anyone could dart out from the stream of pedestrians whilst the Time Portal was open. This was easier said than done and they were on the point of returning home when the pavement became clear, except for a man with a walking stick in the distance. Quickly, Casina walked the short distance to the restaurant door and stepped into the entrance.

She found herself standing on a sandy beach which turned into pebbles, rocks and boulders higher up. Half a mile inland, the rocky surface came up against a small cliff that petered out about half a mile further down.

A small dinghy had been dragged up on to the beach a little way off and tied to a large rock. All this she absorbed in a sweeping glance and her eyes came to rest on the only green object in this barren landscape. It lay close to the cliff and appeared to be a small hillock. However, it moved fractionally from time to time, which was puzzling.

As she scrutinised the mound she realised she was looking at a green dragon which, fortunately, gave the appearance of being fast asleep. Its large head lay on the ground between scaly forelegs, and its eyes were shut. Casina would have been in a state of great agitation at this stage were it not for the fact that she had surmised this must be the very Green Dragon of which Steve had spoken, and which he had described as being very sick.

However sick a dragon might be, she decided she was going to give this one a wide berth, so she turned to walk along the beach in the direction of the small sailing dinghy she had espied tied to a large rock. The sun was high and shone fiercely out of a blue sky. This would be Paradise Casina thought, if only there was some sign of life. "What a barren place this is." Casina said out loud.

"It wasn't always like this." Out from behind the boulder popped a small boy.

Casina stared at him in astonishment.

"You scared me first you know, appearing like that out of nowhere." He replied truculently.

"I am sorry. I am Casina and I don't know where I am. I have come through a Time Portal from another place."

"Oh." He paused. "I am Kez. Our land was green once, I am told, but ever since the Green Dragon became ill – a long time ago – the rains come less often and there is less and less to eat."

"Do you know why the Dragon became ill?"

"One of our stories says he first became sick when St Patrick killed all the snakes. Recently, the dragon has become even weaker. We don't know what to do. The story says..." And here, he looked shyly at Casina.

"Please go on," Casina replied encouragingly.

"When the Seven Islands sing, the 8th Note can be struck at the Heart; the Green Dragon will be restored to health and Heaven and Earth will come together."

"That's interesting. It reminds me of the old Mummer's plays at mid-winter. Someone called St George kills the dragon with his sword but then the doctor comes along and administers pink medicine to the dragon who comes back to life."

Casina pondered awhile. She could see there must be a connection with this legend and the battered xylophone. She took the instrument and the mallet from her pocket and handed them to the boy, who promptly sat down on the sand and played each note in turn.

He grinned. "Do you think that each island is one of these notes? When we have struck each of them can we go in search of the 8th in the middle of the big island?"

Casina laughed. "I do. And, yes, I think we should go in search of the 8th note." She revealed to him how she had been sent by her friend Steve to help heal the Green Dragon and that the legend fitted the hints she had been given on how to achieve this.

Kez jumped to his feet. "I can take you to the islands. I am a good sailor and have visited all of the islands in my boat. Let me take you? Please? They are not far apart. It will only take us three days at the most and my parents won't worry. They will think I am staying with my uncle who is a fisherman."

A little reluctantly at first, Casina agreed to this wonderful offer of help. Ample provisions were already stowed away in the boat and Kez said he knew of a stream on one of the islands where they might replenish their water supplies.

A light breeze was blowing as they set off in a westerly direction along the south coast so that the small boat sped along. Casina could see that Kez was a confident sailor and

handled the boat with ease. Very soon, the first island came into view.

The plan was a simple one. They would go ashore at each of the islands, find a boulder – which, in a manner of speaking resembles a written musical note – and strike it with the mallet to set the stone singing. They were going to visit the islands in the sequence they appeared from their point of departure. This would take them nearly full circle as the last of the seven islands was nearly half-way down the eastern side of the main island.

Casina was trailing her fingers in the water thinking of nothing in particular when the well-known expression, 'The Seven Year Itch', popped into her mind unbidden. In one of those flashes of insight, she understood its meaning. She was sure the well-known expression came from how long it takes the planet Saturn to travel around the sun, which is approximately 28 years. Thus to make a quarter of that circle is seven years. Seven years is therefore 90°.

Astrologers will tell you that it is around the age of 28/29, when Saturn has made one complete circle and is back where it started, that people become serious, take stock of their lives and make changes. 'The Seven Year Itch' corresponds to 90° of Saturn's 28-year cycle. The transition from one period of seven years to the next will cause a similar urge for change in one's life, if perhaps less strong, which gives us that itchy feeling!

In a different way, they were repeating what she and the Arab had done on the tip of the Great Pyramid when she turned the Heart Key through 90°. The aim was similar; to raise the Earth's vibration, or frequency.

As the unpromising coastline of cliffs and jagged rocks drew closer, Casina wondered where they could possibly find a landing place. Kez was unperturbed. Before long, they rounded a promontory and a small sandy beach came into view. They dragged the boat a little way up the beach. Next, Casina handed the mallet to Kez and told him to strike the nearest rock he could find. Without a word, he ran along the beach to a large round rock, which he struck confidently. They set sail once again and repeated the same routine for all seven of the islands.

"Now where do we go?" Kez asked. He picked up the small child's xylophone and played each of the seven notes in turn but did not strike the 8th key. The note hung in the air, as if unfinished, waiting for the 8th note and, at that moment, they both understood the importance of striking the last note. It gave completion.

"Kez, do you by any chance know where the centre of the big island is and, if so, how we might get there?"

"I think I do." Kez replied uncertainly, and pondered the question for a moment.

"I have heard people talk of the Rainbow Waterfall in the middle of the island, high in the Green Hills. That is the only place I can think that might be the centre you are looking for."

Casina was thinking of the rainbow colours on the xylophone, which made Kez's suggestion highly promising.

"I think we should make for that waterfall, Kez. It sounds like just the place where the heart of the island might be. Is it very far away? Would you know where to land?"

"If we continue sailing south down the east coast we will come to the mouth of the East River. It isn't far. We can stow the boat and set off on foot. All we have to do then is follow the river which will take us to the Rainbow Waterfall."

"Okay, let's do it but you don't have to make the journey on foot with me if you would rather go home. Your parents might be worried about you by now." However, Kez was determined to go with Casina, explaining he had to see things through to the end.

Once again, they set sail and it seemed like no time before Casina saw a river delta appear in the distance. The boy had an expert eye for where to land his craft safely. They hid the small dinghy in amongst some bushes, filled Kez's rucksack with supplies and set off on their hike to the fabulous sounding waterfall.

The river, whose course they were following, was a shadow of its former self. Even the surrounding wetlands looked parched. They trekked for several days, climbing ever higher into the woods that cloaked the hills. On the third day they caught their first sighting of the White Hart, a flash of white glimpsed amongst the trees, so that at first, they wondered what on earth it was. From then on, however, if they faltered, the mythical beast would appear as if guiding them to The Falls.

The climb had been getting ever rockier and steeper when, all at once, they emerged onto a large flat rock and found themselves looking across a wide pool beneath them, stretching to an immense cliff face with water flowing over.

Surely, this could not be the fabled Rainbow Waterfall? The waters fell mutely into the pool below and there was a palpable feeling of melancholy in the air. However, the presence of the White Hart, standing fully in the open on a rock close by The Falls, told them that these were indeed they. The waters should have been thundering into the pool below and the rainbow colours should have been hanging suspended in the air as the light caught the exultant spray.

"That must be the 8th note!" and Kez pointed at the rock where the White Hart was standing still. Casina nodded in agreement. They both turned into the trees to follow the edge of the pool round to the rock. When they emerged close to the rock at the foot of the Waterfall the White Hart was nowhere to be seen.

"Go on, Kez. You are lighter and more agile than me."

Kez scrambled over the intervening rocks before levering himself up on to the large flat rock where they had seen the White Hart. He struck the rock with the mallet. A second later, they felt a tremor run through the earth beneath them.

Kez returned with shining eyes.

"Do you think the Green Dragon is healed now?"

"We had better get back and see."

The return journey, naturally, was quicker and easier. As they were about to push off in the boat, they noticed rain clouds gathering in the distance and Kez became very excited.

"It's worked. The Dragon must be better!"

To which Casina replied. "I hope it doesn't rain while we are at sea."

That concentrated Kez's mind and he hurriedly hoisted the sail.

They were only just in time. As they pulled the boat up on to the beach, the sky had turned black and the first heavy drops of rain were beginning to fall. A large crowd had already gathered further up the beach at a respectful distance from the Green Dragon who was stomping about and flapping his enormous leathery wings. A man and woman broke away from the crowd and began running towards them.

"Those are my parents." Kez called out happily.

Casina realised it was time for her to leave.

"I have to go home as well Kez. Thank you for coming with me: I couldn't have done it without you." Impulsively Kez hugged her, then turned and ran up the beach towards his mother and father.

Casina began walking in the opposite direction, towards the Portal, all the while staring in amazement at the enormous dragon. It appeared to be in good shape again. A shimmer in the air became visible and Casina walked back into her own world, confident in the belief that she and Kez had been successful in restoring the health of the Green Dragon and, hence, the health of the land.

Casina met up with Steve at the usual park bench overlooking the river and water meadows. She told him about the chance meeting with Kez, and the prophesy that when the seven islands sang together, the eighth note at the Heart might be struck and the Green Dragon restored to health. She told him of their sea voyage and how they saw that rare creature, the White Hart, which guided them.

When Casina had finished her story, Steve remarked that there was one piece of the puzzle she had omitted – that heaven and earth would meet. This had occurred after she left that country. A great storm had broken soaking the land with water and turning it green once again. As the storm abated, the black clouds parted and a shaft of white light struck the Green Dragon causing it to let out an enormous bellow. So that part of the legend came true as well.

THE END

Made in the USA
Monee, IL
08 July 2026